No good deed goes unpunished.

When an explosion lays waste to part of the city of Toulouse and the citizens attempt to recover in the ravaged cityscape, Louis runs to the aid of people in need.

Chivalrous intent clashes with nefarious goals as Louis has to save himself and those he loves.

R.W. WALLACE
AUTHOR OF THE GHOST DETECTIVE SERIES

THE
RED BRICK
HAZE

A TOLOSA MYSTERY

The Red Brick Haze
by R.W. Wallace

Copyright © 2016 by R.W. Wallace

Copy editing by Leah Wohl-Pollack of Invisible Ink Editing
Cover by the Deranged Doctor Design

All characters and events in this book, other than those clearly in the public domain, are fictitious and any resemblance to real persons, living or dead, is purely coincidental.

All rights reserved. No part of this publication may be reproduced, distributed, or transmitted in any form or by any means, including photocopying, recording, or other electronic or mechanical methods, without the prior written permission of the publisher, except in the case of brief quotations embodied in critical reviews and certain other noncommercial uses permitted by copyright law. For permission requests, write to the publisher, addressed "Attention: Permissions Coordinator," at the address below.

www.rwwallace.com

ISBN: [979-10-95707-41-7]

Main category—Fiction
Other category—Mystery

First Edition

14 13 12 11 10 / 10 9 8 7 6 5 4 3 2 1

Also by R.W. Wallace

Mystery

The Tolosa Mystery Series
The Red Brick Haze (free)
The Red Brick Cellars
The Red Brick Basilica

Ghost Detective Shorts (coming soon)
Just Desserts
Lost Friends
Family Bonds
Till Death
Common Ground

Short Stories
Hidden Horrors
Critters
Gertrude and the Trojan Horse
First Impressions
Out of Sight
Two's Company

Science Fiction (short stories)
The Vanguard
Quarantine (Lollapalooza)
Common Enemies (Lollapalooza)

Adventure (short stories)
Size Matters

Fantasy (short stories)
Morbier Impossible
Unexpected Consequences

ONE

September 21, 2001

A FRAGRANT, BLANKETING smell of runny Roquefort and rank goat cheese blew out of the *fromagerie*'s open door as Louis strolled past, trailing behind his friend Emilie. Louis drew in a deep lungful, enjoying the way the heady mix obscured the stench of exhaust from passing cars. A line of cheese enthusiasts crowded the tiny shop and bled onto the sidewalk, proving that the wares must have tasted as good as they smelled.

He passed into the shadow of a truck unloading goods into a hardware store, and the Saint-Michel Prison came into view. Louis tugged his black-and-white checkered scarf tighter around his neck. The towering building was an architectural beauty—a five-pronged star shape when seen from above and a medieval castle-like entrance, all in red brick to blend in with the other buildings of Toulouse—but it was still a stark reminder of the dark side of humanity. Louis hoped his father would be able to come through on his electoral promise to move the prisoners to a newer and safer facility, releasing the building to be enjoyed by the entire city as a cultural center.

Toulouse had grown incredibly quickly over the last fifty years, and what had originally been a suburb was now a central and very hip neighborhood. What was a decrepit prison doing taking up so much of the sought-after space? Louis's father had proposed converting it to student housing, but Louis had argued that the students spent enough time locked inside classrooms as it was. They shouldn't be living in an old prison, no matter how quaint.

Emilie skipped along the wide sidewalk ahead of Louis, twirling into a pirouette to avoid an oncoming bike; as she spun, her cute yellow sundress flared out like a sunflower and the buttons on her back glinted like diamonds in the morning sunlight. With her cherubic face lit up by an enviable inner joy and sky-blue eyes that danced with cheerfulness, she appeared years younger than her actual twenty. Her diminutive height and tendency to skip rather than walk didn't help in the least. Louis smiled wryly into his scarf at a memory of her, kicking his ass a week earlier when he'd told her she looked sweet.

"Are you sure you won't get in trouble for skipping class?" Emilie glanced up at Louis out of the corner of her eye.

As a car honked at a cyclist who was taking up too much of the narrow street, Louis gave an insouciant shrug. "Why should I get in trouble? Less than half the class ever shows up to Fluid Mechanics anyway. I can't take another hour of that never-ending equation." The class should have been named Quantum Mechanics—the teacher had definitely found a way to stop time.

"I don't think it's just one equation." Emilie didn't appear fully convinced of her own statement.

"Yes, it is. He started that first lesson by lulling us into believing the subject would be interesting, talking about channels and water and stuff. Then he attacked the integrals, and I honestly think that proof is going to take a few months."

Louis glanced back at the looming prison. It mirrored how he felt when he sat in that lecture hall: stuck in a stern and unforgiving place when there were so many better things he could be doing.

"We're better off here, making sure you can go to karate training tonight."

Emilie rolled her sparkling blue eyes at him before jumping over a pothole in the street they were crossing. "It's really nice of you to come with me, Louis, but I'm sure they could have lent me a karategi for the first training session."

They were walking back to campus along a straight, widening axis leading out from the city center. Small specialized shops lined the street, and tables took up most of the sidewalk in front of the cafés. Louis loved the eclectic mix of shops; it perfectly represented his vision of the city of Toulouse.

"What kind of black belt shows up to training without gear?"

Emilie did another little pirouette and winked at Louis. "The kind that worked out just before leaving, and put the gear in the wash out of habit." Cocking her head and smiling with a single dimple, she held up her shopping bag. "But now I'm all set. And you're behind in Fluid Mechanics."

"You didn't need to buy me anything, though." Louis let his hand slide through the folds of his scarf again, enjoying the silky feel of the fabric and the slight pull at the back of his neck.

"You looked like a five-year-old at a teddy bear display when you saw it in the shop," Emilie teased. "How could I not get it for you?"

Spotting a teashop, Louis pulled Emilie with him to the store window. "I just need to go in here for a second. I promised Maman I'd buy her tea some time ago, and I haven't gotten around to it yet." And in case she learned of his skipping class, it would be a good idea to come home with a peace offering. The shop was tiny and cozy, and the fruity and spicy aromas of teas and *tisanes* of all kinds hit them as they entered. They left the front door cracked open as they walked through, letting the busy noise of passing cars interrupt the calm haven.

"*Bonjour*, Madame," Louis greeted the store owner.

The woman never got a chance to answer. As she opened her mouth in a wide smile, the ground started shaking. A second later, a great boom sounded.

Louis looked into Emilie's stunned face. "What was that?" they both said. He stepped back to look out the front door.

There was a change of pressure and his ears popped, a fraction of a second before the door was blown open. Right into his face.

Two

Louis woke up to Emilie's big blue eyes staring into his own from no more than a hand's width away.

"Oh, thank God. You're alive." Her voice sounded like it came from the next room. She exhaled forcibly, then focused on Louis's forehead.

"What happened?" Louis croaked. As he registered the spicy aromas, he remembered where he was: lying on the floor of the tea shop. The glass door—now sans glass—swung loose on its hinges. Louis's ears didn't seem to be working correctly; it was like he was underwater.

Emilie took a handkerchief out of her back pocket and pressed it to Louis's head. "Stay still," she said. "You got a cut when the door hit you." She was yelling now, making the volume just right.

"I got hit by the door?" Louis yelled back.

Emilie nodded and wiped a hand across her dust-covered face. "Whatever that blast was, it had a hell of a momentum. It looks like several windows of the shop next door were blown to bits, too."

Louis tried to get up, but his head wasn't more than a few centimeters off the floor before his vision started swimming.

Emilie pushed him back down. "Don't move. I'm going to call the fifteen. Here." She put one of Louis's hands onto the handkerchief on his head. "You're not bleeding much, but hold that in place."

Louis huffed, but didn't put up much of a fight. He started to become aware of the cut on his forehead, and the tingling in his arms made him suspect he might have more than just the one injury. If his head had collided with the swinging door and caused the glass to break, he must have gotten bits of broken glass in other places, too.

What had happened? At first, when the ground shook, Louis had thought it might be an earthquake—though there were never earthquakes in this region, at least, not ones so strong that they could actually be felt. Plus, an earthquake wouldn't create a blast like that. "Did the Physics department blow up or something?" he wondered out loud.

"Chemistry department sounds more likely," Emilie replied from the other side of the room. Moving his head ever so slightly, Louis spotted her behind the desk of the tea shop, with the phone to her ear. "Though I don't think they have what it takes to make that kind of screw-up. It's a bit far, isn't it?"

"Yeah." Images of the terrorist attack on the Twin Towers flitted through Louis's mind—that had only been ten days ago. Was off-the-beaten-path Toulouse the next target? Could they have targeted Airbus? But that was even farther away than the university.

Slamming the phone back on the receiver, Emilie growled, "All the lines are busy. I can't get through." She stepped carefully across the debris to reach Louis's side, brushing dust from her dress.

"What happened to the shop owner?"

Emilie rolled her eyes. "She shrieked when the door hit you and ran out the back." She studied Louis's eyes. "Can you get up, do you think? There's a bar just next door. We could go in there to see if they know what happened. And maybe find a drunk doctor or something."

Chuckling, Louis nodded. "Let's take it slow. I should be okay."

With copious help from Emilie, Louis made it to his feet. Glass tinkled as it fell from him to the floor. Louis brushed both hands over his scarf to get out any stragglers. He coughed as a cloud of dust formed around him, then buried his face in his scarf, brushing his hands over his clothing to clean up as much as he could.

He had to close his eyes for a moment to make his head stop spinning, but once it had settled, he took in his surroundings. It made him think of Christmas: a million pieces of sparkling broken glass from the front door mingled with the reds, greens, and browns of overturned boxes of tea. Only the thick layer of dirt broke the spell of the scene. "What's with the dirt? Was it blown in with the blast?"

Emilie pointed above the window. "I think the blast blew the dust out of the ventilation. Probably accumulated over God knows how many years. After you fell, there was like a carpet of dirt that glided down from the ceiling."

"Charming."

With Louis holding on to Emilie's shoulder for support, they made their way outside. They gaped at the devastation in the street in front of them. The windows of about half the shops on their side were broken. In the middle of the road, two cars had crashed. Had the blast sent them into each other, or had the drivers lost control of their vehicles? Regardless, all traffic had effectively stopped. People were stepping out of their cars and the shops, looking around in all directions, searching for the cause of the blast.

Louis squeezed Emilie's shoulder. "Let's go into the bar, like you said. They should have a TV in there at least."

"Yeah. And maybe their phone can get through to the fifteen."

Given the state of this street and the fact that the source of the blast was still unknown, Louis had a feeling he wasn't the only person in Toulouse in need of first aid today. With just a few scratches here and there, and that annoying cut trickling blood into his eyes, he would be fine with a bandage or two.

The bar had less than ten patrons, all of whom had eyes glued to the TV screen above the counter. It was tuned to the local news channel, which showed interviews of people in the Toulouse city center.

"Do you know what happened?" Louis asked the bald barman as he sat down in a chair along the bar.

Never taking his eyes off the screen, the barman shook his head. "Nobody has a clue. They're going around the city asking people their opinions, but nobody knows anything."

Louis was about to ask if the man had a first aid kit, but the thought left his head as the next interviewee on TV spoke: "I saw a plane going down on the Capitole. The whole building went up in flames."

Louis's first thought was of his father. Was he at work at the Capitole today? Did he have any meetings? Again, images of the tragedy at the Twin Towers less than two weeks earlier flashed through his mind. Could it really be happening again?

The barman huffed. "Right. The terrorists might be good enough pilots to aim for high-rise buildings, but there is no way anyone could aim for and hit a two-story building that looks identical to all its neighbors from above on the first attempt. Might as well say we've been invaded by martians."

The man had a point. As the next person on TV gave his own explanation for whatever had happened, Louis drew a relieved sigh. His father was okay. He had been mayor of Toulouse for less than two years, but, given his popularity, Louis was ready to bet this wouldn't be his only term of office.

Louis tapped the barman on the shoulder. "Excuse me. You wouldn't happen to have a first aid kit?"

The bald man took his first real look at Louis and started. "*La vache*. What happened to you?"

"I took a door to the face."

The barman stared at Louis's face for a few seconds before springing into action. "I should have something in the back. Give me a minute."

As the man walked into a back room, Emilie jumped up and lay across the bar. She reached for the phone. At Louis's startled expression, she explained, "I'm sure he won't mind. I'm going to try the fifteen again." Once she'd dialed, she let her feet slide back to the floor and stood, receiver in hand.

The barman came back with a decently sized first aid kit. "We keep this in case there are fights. It doesn't happen often, but when it does, it's better to be prepared." He eyed Emilie hugging his phone. "The lines aren't working. There's no point in trying to call your family, *ma petite dame*."

"Call me small again, and I'll kick your ass," Emilie hissed.

The barman was clearly close to laughing out loud at this sweet little girl threatening to kick his bulky ass, so Louis decided to intervene before a real bar fight started. "I'd take that threat seriously if I were you, Monsieur. She has a black belt in karate. And she took me down in about three seconds the first time we met two weeks ago."

The barman barked a short laugh. At least now it was directed at Louis and not the volatile Emilie. The girl was usually sweet and funny, but her size was obviously a sore spot.

"*Oui, bonjour*," Emilie shouted into the phone. She'd gotten through. "I need you to come immediately. My friend was knocked out by a swinging door and is bleeding all over the place."

Exchanging a wary look with the barman, Louis looked down at himself. There *was* blood everywhere. Some spots on his worn jeans, probably blood that had dripped down from his forehead. The scratches on his arms. And a very slow trickle was making its way down his chin. Louis took a step to the side to look at himself in the mirror behind the bar.

Three gashes crisscrossed his forehead. Two appeared to be from the impact of the door. The third must have been a glass cut. Thank God the glass hadn't landed in his eyes. Two lines of blood made their way down his face, one on each cheek. It did look dramatic, but apart from a budding headache and ringing ears, Louis felt fine.

Emilie huffed into the phone before giving her name and the address of the bar. "Now will you come? It's the mayor's son. You can't let him die."

"I'm not exactly dying here, Emilie," Louis said.

"You don't know that." Then she talked back into the receiver. "Yes, he's breathing. Yes, he's standing up. I think he's in a normal state of mind—he's as annoying as ever." A pause. "You're too busy?" The last word came out as a screech.

Louis snapped the receiver out of Emilie's hand and gave her a stern look when she moved to take it back. This was not the time to take him down with karate moves. It was funny at the party two weeks ago—it would be much less so now. "This is the injured man speaking," Louis said into the receiver. "I'm really not severely injured. I'm sure there are other people who need your help more, so I'll hang up now. By the way, you don't happen to know what just happened in Toulouse?"

The woman on the other end of the line replied in the negative. Louis thanked her for her time and hung up.

Emilie's face was beet red, and her blue eyes stared icy daggers at Louis.

"Calm down, Emilie." Louis left no trace of a smile on his face. Normally he was all for fooling around, but this was turning into a most abnormal day. "This is not the time to be offended because someone told you they had more important things to do."

Emilie spoke through gritted teeth. "You need medical care."

"And I'll get it. Right now we're going to go through this man's first aid kit." He nodded at the barman, who'd gone back to watching the TV. "Then, if you want, we can go see if we can find a doctor nearby to have a look at my head."

Emilie clearly wanted to keep fighting, but Louis's logic got through. He watched as she concentrated on calming herself down with a breathing exercise. "Fine," she said once her face was back to its normal color. She grabbed the first aid kit and together they took a seat at a table by the window. Louis suffered his friend's ministrations—not so much because he thought he needed it, but because she clearly did.

With the worst of the blood cleaned off his face and an enormous bandage covering his entire forehead, not to mention numerous small ones on his arms, Louis returned the first aid kit to the barman. "Thank you very much, Monsieur." He pointed at the TV. "Do you know what happened yet?"

"Nope." The man kept his eyes on the screen. "Even the national channels are starting to talk about it, but right now there are a thousand different theories."

Louis and Emilie left the bar in search of a doctor.

Three

Not being familiar enough with this part of the city to know where any doctors might be, they started walking toward campus.

The blast seemed to have impacted the whole city. Everywhere, cars were stopped in the middle of the street and the sidewalks were covered with broken glass and toppled garbage cans. The uninjured were taking care of the injured, though Louis was relieved to see that, at least for the moment, there were no injuries more severe than his own. He was not the only one to regularly shake his head or shove a finger in his ear because his hearing was not yet back to normal. He was beginning to realize that his ears might actually be in worse shape than his forehead.

As they passed in front of an abandoned red brick building, Louis thought he heard someone swear. He looked around, but there was nobody in close proximity. "Did you hear that?" he asked Emilie.

"Hear what? It feels like my ears have been underwater since the blast."

"I think I heard someone swear. Do you think maybe someone's stuck or something?" Louis stopped to look up and down the street. Then he heard a voice again—it seemed to be coming from inside the decrepit building. It was too low for Louis to make out the individual words, but there were definitely at least two men inside.

"How did they get in there?" Louis wondered out loud, eying the sealed-up door and windows of the ground floor. Surely nobody would be crazy enough to climb in through the broken windows on the second floor.

Emilie had her ear to the gray bricks filling the doorway. "You're right. There's someone in there. And they don't sound happy."

"Let's walk around to the back to see if there's another way in." Louis led the way down the narrow side street. On this side, there were no openings to the house at all: it was solid red brick. When they reached the back of the house, they discovered a cobblestone wall that reached to Louis's shoulders.

"The windows on this side are sealed shut, too," he said. Emilie looked like she was debating whether she'd prefer to jump up and see for herself or let Louis do the scouting. "But there's a door. It's bolted. From the outside."

A tiny wrinkle appeared on Emilie's forehead. "Then how did those guys get in there? Do you think they've been imprisoned by someone?"

"I don't know, but I think we should go have a look. The house doesn't look like it's in good shape. Who knows what that earthquake, or whatever it was, could have done?" He gave Emilie a wary look. "Do you want a hand over the wall?"

Emilie leveled Louis with a blank look and kept her eyes on him as she dropped her bag on the sidewalk, jumped, grabbed the top of the wall, and turned so she was sitting on top, legs dangling. "Do *you* need help?" she asked sweetly.

"Yes, please. That would be great." Louis put a foot on one of the cobblestones, grabbed the top with both hands, and inelegantly pulled himself up so he was lying on top of the wall on his stomach. He pivoted, letting his legs swing down on the other side and let himself slide down to the abandoned garden. "What do you know? I didn't need help after all."

Rolling her eyes, Emilie swung her feet across the wall and jumped down with the elegance of a ballerina. "Let's have a look at that door."

They traversed the hard-packed dirt yard, skirting dead bushes and stepping on rare patches of green, until they reached the barred door. Louis rattled the heavy lock. "It's probably locked from the outside because they didn't want anyone to squat. It's been there a while, though. Check out all the rust." He pointed to the bolt where the padlock was attached. The lock itself looked sturdy, but not the support.

Louis gave it a tentative pull. "I don't think it will take much to rip it off." He glanced at Emilie. "What do you think?"

"I can still hear them in there and they're not sounding any happier," Emilie replied. "Go for it."

Taking a good hold of the padlock, Louis adopted a wide stance and pulled with all his might.

The lock and bolt flew off the door. In his surprise, Louis let it slip through his fingers and it sailed into the garden.

"Huh." Emilie studied the place where the bolt had been attached. "They must have installed it mostly for show. A kid could have ripped that thing off."

"Maybe I'm just really strong."

Emilie snorted. "It took a person half your size less than ten seconds to beat you into submission."

"You're a black belt!"

"And you should stay out of fights."

Shrugging, Louis reached for the door. With his gentle push, it opened inward, giving off a quiet squeal.

"Hello?" Louis said into the house. The inside was in an even worse state than the outside. The second floor seemed to have been missing for a while—the whole place was one great open space, going all the way up to the roof. Two broken windows on the second floor brought some light into the gloom. A couple of tiles were missing from the roof, allowing a few rays of light to cut through the decrepit space like headlights through mist.

Of course, what looked like mist was actually dust and dirt. As in the tea shop, the blast had probably blown it around, and it hadn't had time to settle yet. Louis and Emilie stood together, watching the dust dance in the light, not wanting to break the spell.

The house was silent.

Four

The sound of a rock—or probably a brick—falling to the floor in the basement broke the enchantment.

Louis took a step through the door to get out of the sun and allow his eyes to adapt to the gloom. "Is there anybody in here?" he called.

Emilie grabbed Louis by the elbow and he jumped.

"What are you doing?" he hissed.

Pointing to the floor in front of Louis's feet, she said, "You were about to take a plunge into the cellar."

She was right. Not two steps ahead of where he was standing, there was a gaping hole in the floor. Except for a small portion around the staircase, this house didn't have any floors at all. It looked like the second story had been removed on purpose, but the one on the ground floor appeared to have fallen in by itself.

"Do you think the blast made the floor collapse?"

Emilie eyed the swirling dust. "It's possible. Which means there could be people trapped down there."

"You're assuming there would have been people hanging out here in the first place. In a house locked from the outside."

"We heard voices."

"So we did." Louis took a tentative step forward to look over the rim of the broken floor into the basement. "But they shut up when I called out. Hello?" he tried again.

A gruff voice sounded from below. "We could use a hand down here."

Sounds of a shush and heated whispers drifted up from the depths of the basement. Louis decided to let them work out their differences before finding a way down. There was no point in risking his neck if he was going to be sent away. He studied the space around him. Making his way across the ledge on his left to reach the still-intact staircase in the opposite corner would probably be the safest route.

The voice that had spoken up earlier shouted out again. "Would you mind coming down here to help? Our friend is stuck under the debris."

"Sure thing," Louis replied. "We'll be right down."

He glanced at Emilie. "I was going to suggest you wait here, but I'm thinking that might not be a good idea?"

"Not if you want to live." She shouldered her way past Louis and onto the narrow ledge. It was, in fact, all that remained of the floor—only a few centimeters were still attached to the wall. "Come on, Saint-Blancat."

By the time Emilie reached the staircase, Louis was only halfway across the ledge. This was one of those moments where being small gave you an advantage. That, or Emilie was just a lot more nimble and confident than him. Step by step, clinging to the wall and wishing he had lizard feet, Louis managed to join his friend without falling to his death on the heap of wooden beams and red bricks below.

From the top of the staircase, they had a better view of the scene below. Two men crouched in a corner of the basement, just below the back door where Louis and Emilie had stood earlier. One of them, a tall, lanky, dark-haired man in his forties, was throwing debris from the heap in front of them toward the center of the basement. The second—a blond, sturdy, thirty-something giant with dirt stains crisscrossing his face—had a third man's head in his lap and was holding his hand. The hand and head were all Louis could see of the third member of the group—the rest was buried under the debris.

The first man studied Louis and Emilie for a second. "Come help us dig him out, will you?"

Louis launched into action. He hugged the wall as he moved down the steps two at a time, while Emilie followed at a more leisurely pace. Stepping carefully so as not to cut himself again on broken glass or slip on a loose brick, Louis made his way over to the desperate men. He let out a relieved breath when he saw that the third man was alive and awake.

Louis wasted no time and began helping the tall man remove bricks.

"He took a beam across the hips," the man explained as they worked. "I'm removing the small stuff first so we can get a hold of the beam and remove it without hurting him too much."

"Great plan," Louis replied. Now that he was basically standing on top of the fallen man, he saw the rotten wooden beam lying across the man's lower body. Though the lamentable state of the beam was surely the reason the whole thing had collapsed in the first place, it had probably also helped cushion the blow somewhat. "I'm Louis, by the way," he said as he threw a parquet lath across the room. His scarf was getting in the way, so he shoved it down the front of his t-shirt. "And this is Emilie."

Emilie, who had just finished her careful crossing of the basement, gave the men a curt nod. They didn't offer their names in return. To keep them straight in his head, Louis named the tall, dark-haired guy Brown. The giant holding his friend's hand was Blondie.

Emilie knelt down next to the fallen man. "How are you feeling?" she asked.

"A house just fell on me," the man said through clenched teeth, taking quick, short breaths. "How do you think I feel?"

Emilie didn't lose a beat. "Like shit, I guess. What I meant was, do you think anything is broken? Can you move your toes at all?"

The man hissed out a frustrated sigh. "I don't think anything is broken, but it hurts so much, I really can't be certain. It feels like a steamroller is sitting on my hips." Noting only now that this man was a redhead underneath a thick layer of grime, Louis dubbed him Red.

"We'll take care of it," Emilie said in a soothing tone, making sure she held the man's gaze. Louis knew only too well how hypnotizing that gaze could be when she gave you her undivided attention. It was how she had completely blindsided him before laying him flat in front of all his friends.

Louis had already been on his fourth drink of the evening, standing on the side of the hole in the ground nicknamed *le trou*, in front of the student housing, when he had had the brilliant idea to address the pretty girl passing by as *ma petite mademoiselle*. As her face reddened, it had enhanced the pretty blue of her eyes, and Louis flashed a smile, thinking she was blushing because she liked him. Then she'd fixed him with that stare, and crooked her finger to get him to come closer. When he leaned in, she'd thrown him into the middle of *le trou*, making the fifty or so students around them stop their conversations and stare.

Luckily for Red, Emilie wasn't out to humiliate him, but to help him. "I'd propose to call the fifteen, but unfortunately—"

"No calling the fifteen," the blond man said. "There's no need for that."

Louis continued to work on clearing out debris with Brown, but he kept a close eye on Emilie and Blondie. The tension was mounting, but why? And why refuse a call to the fifteen? Their friend was clearly suffering. But the man lying with his head in Blondie's lap, struggling with the pain of each breath, didn't contradict his comrade.

Trying to keep from staring, Louis studied the three men. Since they were inside a decrepit and abandoned house, he'd assumed they were squatters. But underneath the dirt and grime they had clearly accumulated from the day's events, these men were clean and well dressed. Brown wore a sweat suit, accompanied by sneakers that had to be brand new. The clean parts of his shoes were white like a wedding dress. Blondie wore pants and a button-down shirt, both almost new. There was something off about the ensemble, but Louis was unable to pin down exactly what.

They had only started to uncover Red from beneath the debris, but he appeared to be wearing worn jeans and a long-sleeved gray shirt. The shirt sported a few holes, either from use or from the recent accident. In any case, they were all dressed in different styles, making Louis wonder what it was they had in common.

Emilie had put a hand on the fallen man's chest, but was staring daggers at Blondie. "You don't want him to be cared for? Even if he hasn't broken anything, he could have internal bleeding. He needs to see a doctor."

"He needs to get out of here, Mademoiselle, and that's all you need to know."

In the interest of stopping the budding fight, Louis said, "Don't worry, Emilie. I'm sure his friends will see to his well-being once they get him out of this mess. In any case, we've already established that calling the fifteen today isn't productive. Maybe we can bring him with us if we find that doctor for me."

With a glance at the bandage on Louis's forehead, Blondie nodded noncommittally.

"There," Brown said as he grabbed the last brick from around his friend and threw it away. "Now we can get the beam."

Emilie changed places with Blondie—both of them attempting to kill the other with their stares, but still taking great care in transferring Red's head from one lap to the other—and Louis and the two men lined up by the beam. Given the state of the wood, they were certain to get splinters aplenty, but this didn't stop any of them from putting all their might into the lift. The beam was by no means a lightweight, but neither were the three men. On the count of three, the beam was in the air.

While the trio held the wood in place, Emilie helped Red roll away from under it. It was less risky than having the carriers move the beam across the room without any sure footing.

Once Red was free, Louis happily lowered the beam back down to the floor. Clapping his hands together to get rid of the dirt, he felt at least four splinters. He'd look at them more closely once they got back out into the sunlight.

"Can you stand?" Emilie asked Red.

Sweat popping out at his temples, Red used Blondie's help to stand, his breathing labored. He was clearly hurting everywhere and had trouble making his legs cooperate, but he made it into an upright position. "Right as rain," he grunted hoarsely.

Emilie's lips pinched together in a grim line as she shook her head. "So I guess you're up to climbing across that ledge to get out now?" She pointed to the remainder of the ground floor above them.

The redhead eyed the staircase, the ledge, and the back door. "*Putain.*"

Five

They spent ten minutes debating whether Red should go up the stairs and try his luck on the ledge, or if they should find a way to get him straight up beneath the back door. Once he'd recouped enough to walk around for a bit and had recovered his breathing, it became clear that the ledge was not an option. He had trouble standing up straight, and his balance left something to be desired.

They decided to build a platform out of the debris and lift him up from there. So began the work of clearing the area under the door, and then stacking bricks in an orderly fashion. The construction was hardly perfect, but Louis thought it should hold them for the short time they would need it.

For the first five minutes, they worked in silence. Then Blondie studied Louis for a moment before asking, "What happened earlier? Did a van crash into the house or something?"

Louis shook his head. "We haven't figured out what it was yet. But it wasn't in the immediate vicinity. All I know is that there was something like an earthquake, followed by a blast that blew out half the windows on this street."

"The earthquake brought the ceiling down on us. That's how he got trapped." He nodded in Red's direction. He was sitting in the corner, having been banned from helping by Emilie.

Louis looked around the gloomy basement. "What were you doing here in the first place?" He added two more bricks to their foundation. They had a solid base of about two square meters now, reaching to knee height. They would build a smaller square in the middle of this one, to give them footing, at about hip height. It should be sufficient to push Red up to the door.

Blondie only shrugged and turned his back to go pick up more bricks.

Instead of bending down to do the same, Louis squinted up at the shell of a house. The man hadn't said they'd fallen down with the floor, so they must have already been in the basement. But after having moved around a good portion of the debris, Louis was confident there hadn't been any furniture down here. It was as empty as the rest of the house. On the side he was standing on, there was nothing—this he was sure of. But he couldn't make out any details on the other side of the room, partly blinded as he was by the sunlight streaming in through the roof, which created a luminous barrier in the middle of the space.

Since the man gave no indication that he planned to answer Louis's question, Louis decided to take a quick tour of the room. He hadn't gone more than three steps before Brown intervened. "Hey!" he yelled. "We're not done here. What do you think you're doing?"

"I just need to stretch my back," Louis replied, massaging his lower back. He continued across the room until he was almost at the rays of light. Once he got past them, he should be able to see what was on the other side.

"Twenty-somethings don't have back pains from lifting a couple of bricks." The man's voice was already much closer behind Louis. The sounds of tumbling bricks accompanied his steps.

Louis passed through one of the rays of sunlight and stepped into the dark on the other side. He had enough time to see that the other half of the room was exactly like the one he'd left— empty, except for broken beams and red bricks—before he was yanked backward by a hand on his elbow.

Louis pulled right back. They were standing directly in one of the rays of sunlight. Despite the halo forming on Brown's head, he looked anything but angelic.

"What's your problem?" His grip on Louis's arm held firm and he leaned close into Louis's face.

"I don't have a problem. I just needed to stretch my legs for a bit."

"You said your back." The man's eyes narrowed.

Louis huffed. "Back, legs, they're all hurting. I needed to take a break."

"Make up your mind, *petit*."

Louis took his time looking the man up and down. None of the trio was particularly fat; in fact, they were all lean and quite fit. Which meant that Louis ought to back down. If he didn't stand a chance against Emilie, he probably wouldn't fare much better against these three.

Lifting his arms, hands out, Louis cracked a smile. "I'm all stretched out now. Shall we go back to work? I'd like to get outside and try to figure out what happened earlier."

For a good ten seconds, the man stayed immobile and studied Louis. He must have come to the conclusion that Louis was harmless, because he let go of his elbow.

Doing his best to hide his relief, Louis darted a quick glance behind him. And in the two seconds before he passed through the ray of light again, he spotted something odd.

In the very back of the room, almost in the corner, a black hole pierced the red brick wall.

A tunnel.

SIX

IN HINDSIGHT, LOUIS realized that he should have kept moving and pretended like he hadn't seen anything, but he wasn't quick enough for that. Instead he asked, "You came in through a tunnel?"

Brown moved with the speed of a rugby scrum half snapping up a ball as he bent down to pick something up off the floor. On his way back up, he grabbed hold of Louis's hand and pinned it behind his back.

Something sharp bit into Louis's hip. "You're going to continue cooperating," Brown hissed in his ear. "Or I'll slice you to pieces."

The man must have picked up a piece of broken glass from the floor—there certainly was enough of it—and was using it as a weapon. What Louis didn't understand was the change of demeanor elicited by his comment on the tunnel.

"*Du calme*," Louis said, making no brusque moves, indicating only submission. "I don't care where that tunnel leads. I doubt the neighbor's reaction to it warrants you taking hostages."

Brown pushed Louis away from the tunnel and the beams of light. "Get moving. I'm going to let you go so you can continue helping us get out of here. But if you try *anything*, I'm taking my weapon to your friend. Don't be stupid and think you can beat us. Even after what he's been through today, my red-haired friend could take down the two of you easily. There are three of us, and only one and a half of you."

Louis knew for a fact that, in a fight, Emilie was worth a lot more than her size indicated, but refrained from saying so to his captor. When the iron grip on his hand let go and the sting of the glass disappeared from his side, he carefully put one foot in front of the other until he reached the rickety construction. With a glance back at Brown—he'd already moved close to Emilie—Louis went back to work.

His mind churned on the possible implications of the man's reaction. First, he wondered if they could somehow have been the instigators of whatever caused the earlier earthquake and blast, but the fact that they had been just as surprised down here as everybody outside ruled that possibility out. Could they be looting people's cellars, using that tunnel? If so, where was the loot? And why was the door to the house locked from the outside? They would hardly bother with such a setup if they went in and out regularly.

As he laid two more bricks on their construction, Louis thought back to the flimsy hinges and the solid padlock on the back door. These men had planned to come through that tunnel and that back door. The setup was there to discourage anybody else from squatting in the abandoned house. And it would only need to be broken once.

Had they robbed a bank, and this was their escape route? It was the most plausible answer Louis could come up with, though he wasn't certain there was a bank nearby. Since there were no bags of money lying around, that would also mean the robbery hadn't taken place yet. Perhaps they were still digging the tunnel. With a bolt on the front door.

Louis shook his head at himself. He wasn't going to figure anything out with his mind going in circles. He might as well keep working and focus on getting away from the three men. One thing was clear: they were bad news.

A rock bounced off Louis's thigh. With a start, he looked up into Brown's dark stare. He was standing just behind Emilie, with one hand hidden inside his sweatshirt pocket. Louis had no doubt Brown still held the shard of glass, and was reminding Louis of the overhanging threat. The man nodded at the brick construction in front of Louis. Time to get back to work.

Emilie seemed oblivious to the situation. She kept a good pace lifting bricks. Once she spared a dark glance at the man behind her, clearly wondering why he wasn't helping out like everybody else. Louis didn't try to apprise her of the situation. He was afraid she might take matters into her own hands. And though she could easily take down Louis, he wasn't confident she'd win against these men. So he gave his friend an encouraging smile and bent down to pick up two more bricks.

They were close to finishing the construction. Just one more layer of bricks and they could all get out of here. And hopefully go their separate ways.

Brown glanced at his watch and flexed his jaw. "That's enough," he said.

Emilie shot another dark look at the man, probably in response to his authoritative tone. When she glanced at Louis, he gave her a curt shake of his head to indicate there was no point in making a scene.

Still standing close behind Emilie, Brown pointed at Louis with his free left hand. "You help with getting our wounded friend out first. I'll follow with Mademoiselle."

Of course. Louis didn't much like the idea of abandoning Emilie, but the three men didn't appear particularly stressed out, so it was unlikely they would actually hurt her as long as he cooperated.

Louis and Blondie moved to the corner to help Red get up. With a hand on each of their shoulders, Red shuffled his way over to the red brick construction. The blond man jumped up the first step. With him pulling and Louis pushing from behind, they managed to get Red one step up. Then they repeated the procedure to get up the second step.

With Louis standing on the newly constructed pedestal—he couldn't help but be satisfied that it appeared quite solidly built—the broken beginnings of the floor by the back door reached his shoulders.

While Red took hold of the wooden beam just below the door, Louis and Blondie each bent down to grab a thigh with one arm and a hip with the other. On three, they lifted the man until he was lying on his stomach halfway over the threshold of the back door.

"I'm out," Red exclaimed. The sheer joy and relief in this statement was so heartfelt, Louis felt sure it was about more than just getting out of the house. In a way, Red sounded how Louis felt when his Fluid Mechanics class finally came to an end.

As curious as Louis was, finding out who these men really were was not as important as getting Emilie, and himself, out of this situation in one piece. Once Blondie had heaved himself up and was helping Red get out of the house, Louis followed suit. Then he stood in the doorway, overseeing Emilie's exit. Perhaps they could make a run for it before Brown came out.

But it seemed Brown had had the same thought. When Emilie made to climb up the construction, he held her back. "I'll go first, Mademoiselle."

Emilie sputtered, but Louis managed to catch her gaze, and she got the message: *Don't complain. Just get out of there once the other guy is finished.*

Naturally, once Brown reached the door, he took his place behind Louis. Again, Louis felt the sting of the shard in his side. The man must have cut a hole in his pocket so that the weapon was out of sight, but just as dangerous. How had he not cut his own hand?

"We just need you to cooperate for a short while longer," Brown whispered in Louis's ear. "Then we'll let you and your friend go."

"Fine," Louis growled. As Emilie nimbly jumped up to push herself out of the old house, Louis asked the man behind him, "What were you doing in that tunnel?"

The glass cut a little deeper. "Don't you worry your pretty little head about that." He stared at Emilie, who was frowning at Louis, clearly catching on that she had missed something. "Off we go, Mademoiselle. If you would please join me and my friends down in the garden?"

SEVEN

THE IVY HAD been abandoned for so long, it had grown to completely hide the door beneath it. By the time Louis, Emilie, and Brown had crossed the sad garden, Blondie had sufficiently cleared the greenery to reveal a shabby metallic door in the cobblestone wall in the far corner of the garden. Blondie took up a steady stance, then launched a violent kick at the door. It flew open and fell off its hinges.

With a significant look at his two friends, he declared, "We're out."

Louis froze. He knew where that tunnel led to.

There were no banks in this neighborhood, but there was a prison.

It was even a well-known fact that there were hidden tunnels underneath the prison; they had been excavated by escaping prisoners during World War II, but the people who knew their exact location were long gone. They supposedly held the corpses of several prisoners who had mysteriously disappeared during the war.

These men had clearly found the tunnels—with or without outside help—and used them to escape.

Brown nodded, but he didn't dwell on their victory for long. "We still need to get out of the city." He gave a little nudge with the shard, which he now held to Louis's midsection. "Do you have a car we can borrow?"

"Ouch!" Louis tried to twist away from the man, but was held back by a hand on his elbow.

"Stay still." Once he was satisfied that Louis wouldn't move again, Brown eased up on the death grip. The shard stayed in place, however, with just enough pressure to hurt.

Emilie watched the exchange between Louis and Brown with narrowed eyes. Her stance shifted from the innocent one she usually affected into the easy posture of a fighter ready to spring into action. Had the other men noticed the change, or did they still only see the yellow sundress?

After a long look at Brown's pocket and the weapon inside it—probably to show the man she knew something was going on there—Emilie fixed her stare on Louis's captor. "He doesn't have a car. And neither do I."

Louis heard the mockery in the man's tone. "And I should believe you just because you said so?"

"Believe me or not. I don't care. But there's no car."

Brown turned to Blondie. "Search them for keys."

Louis wondered what the men were in prison for. If they had taken the chance on escaping, it must've been something bad enough to merit a long sentence. Louis decided he'd rather not know. He and Emilie just needed to get away from them, and let the police take care of the trio.

Louis saw the calculation of odds going on behind Emilie's eyes. There were three of the men—though one was severely incapacitated—and two of them. She was a good fighter. She couldn't know what kind of weapon Louis was being threatened with, but she probably assumed the worst.

Louis didn't want her to start a fight. If Louis's deduction that they were prisoners was correct, who knew what they were willing to do to bring their plan to fruition? All three were clearly in good shape, and desperate.

He caught her gaze and signaled with his eyes as best he could that there was no point in fighting. Let them search. After all, there really were no car keys.

With a sullen look in Louis's direction, Emilie sighed. "Fine."

"You try *anything* and this situation changes radically," Louis warned Blondie as he approached Emilie.

The man snorted and changed directions to stand close to Louis—so close that the tips of their shoes were touching. With his lip curling into something between a sneer and a smirk, he said, "What kind of *anything* are we talking about here? This?" He reached around to slap his hand on Louis's back pocket. "No keys there."

Louis froze, feeling like a porcupine with the hairs on the back of his neck and arms standing on end. He couldn't have moved to save his life; he just stared into the amused face of the other man.

Blondie shifted slightly to slap a hand on Louis's other back pocket. "Ah, got something." He fished out Louis's wallet and held it up with a fake self-satisfied grin. "Let's see…" He quickly rifled through it and extracted a hundred-franc bill. Then he held the wallet in a mock salute. "Thank you." He also pulled out Louis's *Carte Bleue*. "I'm guessing it won't do us much good without your pin code, but I'll be taking this too."

He put the wallet back in Louis's pocket, taking care to give it a little extra pat, pretending to make sure it was secure, keeping eye contact with Louis the entire time. Louis got the feeling the man was enjoying his reaction to this process immensely.

"I thought you were looking for keys." Emilie's voice dripped with scorn.

Blondie flashed a big-toothed smile. "Oh, right. Well, let's see then."

Louis braced himself as Blondie's hands approached his front pockets, his heart thudding in his chest.

"Do you have anything in here?" Blondie asked, his hand hovering just above Louis's front pocket.

Though he understood that the man thrived on Louis's discomfort, Louis couldn't help gulping before replying in a whisper, "No."

"No?" Blondie sent a pitying glance down Louis's front. "Really? Nothing?"

Louis felt a blush rising in his cheeks. He heard nothing but the thudding of his own heart as he became unnervingly aware of the smell of clean sweat from Blondie in front of him and Brown behind him. Two people were in his personal space, and he hadn't invited them in.

Blondie wasn't done, though. "See, I believe you when you say you have nothing down your pants. I really do. But if there's one thing I've learned over the past years, it's that you can never take a man at his word." He put his hands on his hips as he shook his head and thinned his lips in mock regret. "I'm afraid I'll have to go in and check."

Emilie spoke up again. "Will you stop playing with him and behave like a professional?"

Blondie huffed. "A professional what? Did you think we were cops?"

Before Emilie could reply, Brown said in a gruff voice, "This has been fun and all, but we need to get going. Especially if we're going to end up walking. Finish the search already."

Blondie flashed a crooked smile at Louis. "I was done playing anyway. It was fun." He finished the frisking rapidly without touching anything he shouldn't have. He fished out Louis's house keys, but slipped them back into Louis's pockets immediately.

Chest heaving, Louis forced himself to look Blondie in the eye, despite the other man's knowing smirk.

"No car keys," the man sighed theatrically before turning to face Emilie. "The search continues."

Still frozen in place, Louis stared at Blondie's back and tried to force himself to think of something other than what had just happened. In France there was no dress code in prisons, as in American movies. The inmates wore whatever they'd brought with them—except for shoes; those had to be bought from inside the prison—or whatever their friends and family could bring them during their stay. Louis again considered the men's clothing, under the hypothesis that they were escaping prisoners. The one with the ragged clothing could have been out of funds for a while, and therefore wore the same shirt he'd worn inside for years. The one with the brand-new sneakers could have made that investment with their escape in mind. And the last man… Louis finally realized what was odd about his clothes: They were about ten years out of fashion. He might have saved the clothes he went into prison with in order to have something presentable for when he found himself outside of those red brick walls.

Louis was brought out of his reverie by an exclamation from Emilie—Blondie had grabbed her thigh while emptying the pockets of her dress.

"What?" Blondie said, oozing innocence. "I was just getting these." He held up Emilie's key chain and jingled it in front of her furious face.

Louis moved to get closer to his friend, but Brown clamped his hand down on Louis's shoulder to keep him in place.

Blondie returned the keys before taking a step back to consider the slight girl in front of him. "There aren't that many places you could hide car keys, are there?" His eyes dropped to her chest. "There's some room in there, I think. Let's see." He raised his hands in a gesture that left no doubt about his intentions.

Louis took a step closer, even managing to ignore the pain as Brown increased the pressure of his weapon against Louis's side, but Emilie moved faster.

Before Blondie's hands even touched her chest, she slapped both arms away, one to each side. With Blondie wide open, she leaned to the side, putting all her weight on one foot, and sent a firm kick straight into the man's chest.

Blondie fell on his ass with a grunt.

Louis tensed. With that piece of glass already cutting into his body, he wouldn't stand a chance if a fight erupted. Even without a weapon, Brown would no doubt be able to beat him into submission in seconds. What could he do? He should probably fight anyway, in order to give Emilie the chance to escape.

But nobody moved. Blondie stayed on the ground, his narrowing eyes on Emilie.

Emilie kept her fighter's stance, but slowly lowered her arms to her sides. "I'm not looking for a fight," she said. "But the search is finished. We don't have any car keys."

Blondie jumped into a standing position, proving he had moves to rival Emilie's. "When a professional searches a woman, he checks the chest."

Louis was amazed at Emilie's calm as she replied, "Yes, but they're searching for illegal substances or weapons. No normal person carries her car keys in her bra. And you said yourself you're not a professional. I will not subject myself to another 'search.'"

Blondie looked like he wanted to continue arguing, but Brown interrupted. "Let's get moving. We'll find a car elsewhere." The sting to Louis's side returned. Was that a drop of blood trickling down his leg? Brown pointed at Emilie with his free hand as he addressed Blondie. "Make sure she doesn't run off, but keep it civil. We don't want to attract anyone's attention."

Gritting his teeth, Blondie complied. He grabbed hold of Emilie's wrist and dragged her behind him out to the street. To anyone not looking closely, they could have been holding hands. Louis was relieved to see Emilie cooperate.

They returned to rue Saint-Michel, where chaos still reigned. Traffic was at a standstill due to several accidents. Alarms made nerve-racking background music. Drivers stood in the street talking, oblivious to having left their keys in the ignition and engines running. Brown eyed several cars that would be only too easy to steal, but quickly came to the conclusion that they wouldn't get anywhere fast.

"What the hell happened?" Brown wondered out loud.

Louis raised his shoulders a fraction to indicate he had no idea. The movement made the sting worse, and he quickly dropped them.

Apparently, the driver of one of the cars they passed had heard Brown's question. Breath catching, he turned in their direction and barely managed to talk through hiccups.

"There was…this big cloud…like a mushroom…over there, behind Pêch David…a nuclear bomb!"

Having delivered the pronouncement, he took off down the street at a dead run.

EIGHT

Louis stared after the man. A nuclear bomb? In Toulouse? Were they all doomed to die within hours? Louis looked down at his bare arms, searching for blisters or whatever wounds a nuclear explosion would cause.

Brown must have had the same thought. He stopped an elderly lady shuffling past them. "*Excusez-moi*, Madame. Is it true? Was there a bomb?"

The old lady squinted at Brown, her mouth opening like a fish out of water as she drew in air to reply. "I don't know about a bomb, young man. But there was a big red cloud in that direction about an hour ago." She pointed in the same direction the madman had earlier.

"It was red?" Louis asked.

"That's what I said, isn't it?" With her wrinkled face folding up into a frown, the lady shuffled away.

Nuclear bombs didn't make red clouds. At least, Louis didn't think so.

Nobody moved as they waited for Brown, the obvious leader of the group, to come to a decision. Blondie used one arm to support Red, who was able to walk somewhat, but was hardly in excellent shape. With his other hand, he kept a firm grip on Emilie, who, for the moment, at least, let herself be dragged along. How were they going to get themselves out of this fix?

Louis addressed his captor. "We could drop by the bar just down there." He pointed at the place they had visited earlier. "There's a TV, and they're watching the news. With more information you could form a viable plan." Plus, Louis might find an opportunity to liberate himself.

Brown stared hard at the bar for a few moments before nudging Louis in the other direction. "I don't trust you. We'll find some other place."

They walked slowly down rue Saint-Michel, letting Red decide the pace and treading carefully around broken glass. It didn't take long for them to find another bar, and, after inspecting it carefully from the outside, Brown led the way in, his weapon still cutting into Louis's side. Red was panting and his skin was pasty just from the five-hundred-meter walk.

Louis could see why Brown would risk going in here. Only three patrons occupied the bar. They all had their backs to the door and were facing the TV behind the counter with their mouths hanging open. The national news broadcast was just starting; the pretty blond anchorwoman looked severely into the camera as she told her viewers that a large explosion had taken place in Toulouse that morning.

Brown kept a firm grip on Louis, but at this point there was really no need. Louis was as glued to the screen as everyone else. Only certain words made their way into Louis's brain, accompanied by apocalyptic images.

"*Poudrerie nationale*…chemical factory…produces fuel for the Ariane rockets…situated in the suburbs of Toulouse…several deaths…" The images were all grey with a pinkish hue—dust, dirt, and concrete covered everything. The ring road, where cars had stopped in whatever place the explosion had sent them. One had a great slab of rock or concrete on the trunk. It was as if a baby god had gotten tired of playing and carelessly tossed the cars and people of Toulouse to the ground. In the area right next to the highway, where the chemical factory had stood, there was only desolation: a gigantic crater and a chimney bent at a thirty-degree angle.

The *poudrerie nationale* produced the powerful fuel used to send the Ariane rockets into space. That stuff *could* blow up half the city. The woman talked about three dead victims, but after seeing the devastation on the screen, Louis knew there would be many more. He agreed with the woman they had talked to at the fifteen: there were people in Toulouse who were in much greater need of medical care than Louis with his scratches.

On the screen, the local TV station took over. A clearly shocked journalist started talking, his eyes wide, his hands gripping the desk in front of him as if he were afraid he might fall off his chair. He'd been close to the explosion when it happened, and had arrived at the scene at the same time as the first responders. As he talked, the video feed of his scooter driving through the scene was shown on screen.

It was oddly reminiscent of the images of the Twin Towers collapsing. Pieces of concrete were everywhere. Firemen were making their way through the industrial site, searching for survivors. The shocked people on the ring road stared into space or at their ruined cars.

The bus depot, which was just next to the factory, was in shambles. Most of the buses had been destroyed. In the Mirail neighborhood, all the windows had apparently been blown to bits by the blast.

The anchorwoman urged the citizens of Toulouse to stay in their homes, for fear of a toxic cloud.

The news report must have lasted less than three minutes, but the impact was tremendous.

Toulouse would never be the same again.

Nine

Louis remembered his father talking about the two factories, the *poudrerie nationale* and AZF, a factory producing nitrogen fertilizer. Both were situated just outside the ring road. They were originally built on the outskirts of town, but with the city growing fast over the last fifty years, they were now well inside city limits. People had been talking about moving them farther out, but the cost was too steep. Now it looked like they'd been right to worry, and the citizens of Toulouse were paying the price.

Louis's father hadn't been mayor long enough to be blamed for this, surely, but how he handled it was sure to affect his future at the Capitole. Louis should be going home, or perhaps directly to the Capitole, to get more information—and to tell his parents he was okay.

Brown swore under his breath. "Looks like we're walking, boys." He locked eyes with Red. "How far can you walk? And how fast?"

Though he was still pale, Red set his jaw and straightened a fraction. "I can walk as far as I have to. That"—he pointed to the screen— "shouldn't stop us from making it to the rendezvous."

"The barman probably has aspirin or something," Louis volunteered, before he could think better of it. Why was he helping these men? They were escaped prisoners, holding him hostage, and Louis had an inkling about at least one of the men's crimes after the way Blondie had groped him and Emilie earlier. Louis told himself to stop being helpful.

Though Red looked hopeful at the idea of a pain reliever, Brown shook his head. "I don't want anyone to remember us." He glanced at his watch again. "Let's go." He waited for Red, Blondie, and Emilie to move out first before he followed.

"Do you really need us to tag along?" Louis asked as they started trudging down the sidewalk in direction of the Saint-Agne neighborhood and the university campus. "Where is your rendezvous?"

"That's none of your business," Brown said. "I don't want you to rat us out, so you're going to stay with us until we find a more efficient mode of transportation."

"It wouldn't even matter if we called the cops," Emilie said. "First, it's near impossible to get through—all the telephone lines are saturated. And second, as the news just clearly illustrated, they have more important things to do today."

Louis grunted an agreement. "They won't care about three measly bank robbers, not today." He planned to wait as long as possible to let the men know he'd deduced why they had really been in that cellar.

With a quick glance that neither Blondie nor Brown noticed, Emilie studied Louis's expression, probably to figure out if he really was that stupid. She must have given him the benefit of the doubt, because she let his statement stand.

Brown shot Louis a threatening, dark look in response to the description. He made no comment, but it was clear he didn't agree with Louis's evaluation that he was a 'measly' anything. Could he really have done something so bad that the police would stop tending to the citizens of Toulouse and go after him instead?

Ten

RED'S TATTY T-SHIRT was soaked through by the time they reached the Saint-Agne train station. Louis had assumed the three men planned to walk out of the city, but when they reached the spot where the road dipped under the railway bridge at Saint-Agne, Brown nudged them all up the concrete stairs and onto the tiny platform.

Both platforms were near empty. A young couple sat close together on a tagged-up bench on the opposite platform, sharing earbuds. Louis first guessed they were listening to music, but given their grim expressions and the looks they exchanged, it was most likely the news.

A little farther down the platform sat an elderly man, clutching two suitcases and looking utterly lost.

Louis thought of the news broadcast telling everyone to stay indoors. How much of the slight breeze he was breathing contained dangerous chemical substances? There was a faint odor that shouldn't be there, but he wasn't able to identify it. Their short walk had brought them closer to the site of the explosion. In fact, the railroad ran straight from this station to the chemical factories. Louis tried to bury his nose in his scarf, in the vain hope that it might do some good.

Brown looked up and down the small station, clearly searching for something or someone.

"I doubt there'll be any trains today," Louis said. "You saw the state the highway was in on the news broadcast earlier; there's no way the railroad tracks are clean enough for the trains to get past."

Brown gave Louis a dirty look. He stared down the tracks in the direction of the chemical factory and winced. He knew Louis was right, but he kept searching. Perhaps it wasn't a train he was looking for.

"Go check inside the station," Brown said to Blondie. "And be quick about it."

Leaving Red leaning against a commercial display, Blondie stalked over to the small waiting room of the railway station, dragging a resistant Emilie behind him. Thirty seconds later, they were back with a wide-eyed and slightly overweight man about Louis's age. "He was cowering in a corner."

Emilie tried to pull her arm free of Blondie's grasp. "Will you let me go? You're cutting off all the circulation to my hand." She tried prying the man's fingers off her wrist with her free hand.

Blondie flicked away her hand and replied, in a tone usually reserved for misbehaving children, "If you stop trying to get away, I'll loosen my grip. It's up to you." His attention returned to the newest member of their group.

"We need to change plans," Brown said to the chubby man. "You must have realized this a while ago. Please tell me you were smart enough to come up with something else in the meantime, and were not just hiding in the corner?"

The newcomer's eyes flew from Brown's face to Blondie's, then to the redhead's, then back to Brown's. He glanced at Louis and Emilie, but said nothing; he was clearly not important enough in this gang to be allowed to ask questions. "I didn't realize it would be that big." His voice shook, and he kept wringing his hands and pulling on the sleeves of his long-sleeved t-shirt.

"What?" Brown said. Louis winced as Brown shoved the shard of glass into his side, but he didn't say anything—he knew it was only in reaction to what the young man had said. "You didn't realize what would be so big?"

The chubby man's lips wobbled and he seemed to be fighting to catch his breath. In the end, his fear of Brown got him talking. "The diversion. It was just supposed to draw the police away."

"That was you?" Brown bellowed, before looking around to check if anybody had heard. He continued, in a more normal voice, "You blew up the *poudrerie nationale*? You were supposed to create a slight diversion, not blow up half the city."

"I did. I—"

"You said you knew what you were doing."

The man was back to pulling on the sleeves of his shirt. "I do. I did. I found a breach in the fence surrounding the factory, and then an isolated electrical cabinet where nobody would see me come or go." He stared beseechingly at Brown. "That site is a high security facility—"

"Of course it is," Brown said through gritted teeth. "Because if something goes wrong, it could *blow up half the city*."

The man swallowed with an audible gulp. "It also means all kinds of security measures should be in place. Some sparks flying in an electrical cabinet should not trigger the whole thing to blow up." His voice gained some confidence as he continued, "A small incident like the one I created should not have spread, but it *should* have made the police come running."

Blondie intervened for the first time. "You are stupid enough to think you could set up a small explosion at the *poudrerie nationale*? Have you seen those rockets when they go off into space?" He tightened his grip on the man's neck, and on Emilie's wrist as well, judging by her wince.

The young man's breath was coming so fast Louis was afraid he might start hyperventilating. "Something happened, and a second explosion was set off by the first one. I swear it wasn't my fault. If they respected all security measures like they should, there would only have been the one small explosion."

Blondie knocked on the man's head, as if trying to physically force his words in there. "You blew up the city using rocket fuel."

The man sent wide-eyed looks around the group. A gleam of hope appeared on his face. "I just messed a little with an electrical cabinet at the *poudrerie nationale*. That's wasn't the factory that blew up; it was AZF. That's not as dangerous."

"I think the state of the city proves that it is dangerous enough." Brown exhaled a great sigh as he shook his head. "Well, you certainly have the police occupied."

Louis shook his head but kept his mouth shut. Now that he thought about it, the chimney he'd seen on the news *had* belonged to AZF, and not the neighboring factory. If the man was telling the truth, and the explosion at the fertilizer factory was enough to blow up so much of the city, what would it have been like if both factories had gone up?

"How come you didn't die in the explosion?" Louis asked. This got him an annoyed sigh from Brown, but luckily, no extra stab in his side.

"I used a timer," the young man answered absently, his eyes now on Red. "I'm going to check on Eric."

Blondie let him go, and the chubby man went to put a hand on Red's—or rather, Eric's—shoulder as he murmured, "It's me. It's Gaël. What happened to you?"

"Okay." Brown turned his back on Eric and Gaël. He seemed to have accepted that they had accidentally blown up half the city, and the only thing that annoyed him was that it had messed up their plans. What had this man gone to prison for?

Everybody looked at each other as they wondered how to get away from the city. Louis tried to silently communicate to Emilie that she should make a run for it, but she shook her head. Louis couldn't make out if that meant she couldn't get away, or that she wouldn't go without him. In any case, they'd have to be on the lookout for an opportunity to run together.

"All right," Brown said in a firm voice. "There won't be any trains today, but the railroad tracks go straight out of the city, to the south. We'll just follow them until we get far enough away for it to be worth it to steal a car."

"They'll take us right past the explosion," Blondie said. "You sure that's a good idea?"

A deep-throated growl emanated from Eric as he slid down the commercial display until he was sitting on the concrete platform. Gaël crouched down next to him, his hand still on Eric's shoulder.

Brown chewed on his lip for a few seconds. "I don't think Eric is coming with us. Does anybody have a problem with that?"

Silence.

"But—" Gaël stood up, and his gaze darted back and forth between the friend slumped at his feet and Brown.

"All right." Brown gave Louis a shove to the edge of the platform. "Off we go. Let's move."

Louis caught Emilie's gaze. Was this their opportunity? He sat down on the edge of the platform and jumped down onto the tracks when Brown told him to. At least for the moment he was away from the shard of glass.

"Go!" Emilie yelled, and attacked Blondie. Using his grip on her arm against him, she barreled into him and all but lifted him up on her shoulders before pitching him onto the railroad tracks.

Louis gaped at his friend's fighting skills for a second, then snapped back to reality and took off running down the tracks. He kept one eye on the fight, not wanting to abandon Emilie.

Her move would have worked to perfection if Blondie hadn't been able to keep his wits about him, even in free fall. He never let go of Emilie's hand, not even to brace himself before hitting the ground. Instead, he used her body weight to right himself in midair and pulled her along with him. The result was such that Blondie landed on his feet and Emilie toppled onto the tracks after him, losing her balance and banging first her head into the large man's chest and then her shoulder against the concrete platform on her rebound.

Ten meters down the tracks, Louis stopped running. He could get away, he was sure of it. But he couldn't just leave Emilie there. She was a strong fighter—much stronger than Louis—but clearly, so was Blondie. Feeling the ghost of the man's hand on his body from the earlier search, Louis felt certain he couldn't abandon his friend, even if her chances of escape were probably better without him. Blondie hadn't gotten what he wanted from her earlier—would he try again if Louis went away?

Blondie grabbed hold of both of Emilie's arms and held them firmly behind her back while Brown, with a dismissive glance at Louis, jumped down next to them. Brown pointed his shard of glass vaguely in Emilie's direction. The movement was casual, but the message was clear enough. "You coming back?" he called to Louis.

Louis returned to the group, his steps heavy.

"Good boy," Brown said, and took up position behind Louis, his weapon once again biting into Louis's skin. Louis's entire right ass cheek was wet with blood now. He didn't think he was bleeding too much, but a small trickle over time would add up.

Gaël came running down the platform toward the group, his eyes still darting back to Eric every few seconds.

"What?" Brown barked.

"I'm coming with you."

Brown gave a sigh. "Why don't you stay here and take care of your friend?"

With another quick glance at Eric slumped on the platform, Gaël scrambled down onto the tracks next to Brown. "He just needs a little rest. Then he can take care of himself."

Brown narrowed his eyes and turned to give Gaël his undivided attention.

"I promised I'd help you guys get away, so that's what I'll do." Gaël's mud-brown eyes were wide with fear. "I've studied your work for years. I know it's not a good idea to cross you."

Brown gave a curt shake of his head. "I just told you it's okay if you stay."

"I'm not taking any chances. Besides, I like to follow through on my promises." Gaël waved a hand southward. "I'll accompany you until you get a car, then I'll come back for Eric."

Brown studied the other man for several moments and a frown appeared on his forehead. Finally, he said, "Suit yourself," and, with a push on Louis's shoulder, began walking along the tracks.

Blondie had a whispered conversation with Emilie, who gritted her teeth and gave a curt nod in reply. He let go of one of her arms, and returned to holding one of her wrists. "Let's go, then," he said, and strode down the tracks after Brown and Louis, toward AZF and the Pyrenees.

They left Eric sitting on the platform. None of his fellow prisoners even said goodbye.

Eleven

Did they realize just how close to AZF the railroad tracks went? There was no way they were getting past the area. Louis kept his mouth shut and continued to search for an opportunity to get away.

As they closed in on the site of the explosion, Louis's mouth went dry. It looked how he'd always imagined a war zone: debris was everywhere, and every inch of the place was coated in a layer of dust and ground-up concrete. The air was a pink-gray haze, and heavy with the pungent smell of ammonia. As they got closer, the cars they passed were in worse and worse condition—Louis was pretty sure one of them held a dead man. Since there was no way Brown would let him go over and see, he looked away and prayed the man had just passed out. The blood trickling out of his ear wasn't too reassuring.

It had taken Gaël about five minutes to walk off his shock; the Saint-Agne train station had still been in view when he'd started talking. Though Gaël never gave any details, Louis surmised the man was a small-time criminal, and Brown was his big hero. It was approximately the way Louis would behave if he met Zinedine Zidane. When Gaël had learned his friend Eric was sharing a cell with his idol, he'd apparently jumped at the chance to help them both escape. Eyes shining, Gaël traipsed along like a five-year-old on his way to Disneyland, with the same capacity for mood change. He ignored Louis and Emilie completely.

"Do you remember that jewelry store?" Gaël gushed. "I can't believe you got away from that one without a scratch."

Brown cut off the beginnings of a growl and hissed at the other man. "Didn't anybody ever teach you when to keep your mouth shut?"

Gaël threw a quick glance at Louis. "Oh, don't worry about him. If they couldn't nail you for it back then, they won't be able to now just because of something I said." He threw his hands in the air as if thanking the gods. "I mean, you robbed that place with two other people and everything that could go wrong *did*. One of your colleagues was caught and is *still* in prison, and the other *died*. And you walked away without a scratch." His breath hitched. "That's class."

"Thanks," Brown grumbled, clearly hoping that was the end of it.

But Gaël was far from done. "I mean, the police come, which would freak anybody out, but do you freeze? No. You don't do like your colleague and give up. But you're not stupid enough to open fire on the officers either." He rubbed a hand on his chest. "You throw down your weapon so the police will *think* you're giving up, but instead of giving yourself over, you grab your other colleague and hide behind her."

"Enough," Brown growled.

"The sudden movement throws everybody off kilter and your colleague accidentally fires her gun. And still you don't panic. No—you just stay behind her, using her as a human shield for when the officers return fire. And in the chaos that follows? You slip away." Gaël heaved a happy sigh. "That's true genius."

Voice clipped and strong, Brown said, "I said, *enough*."

Gaël's step faltered, and, though he quickly recovered, he stopped talking.

Twenty minutes later, they'd put the worst of the disaster behind them, stepping over chunks of debris, red bricks, and pieces of concrete. They soon arrived at something resembling a small train station. It was clearly not in commercial use, but perhaps the factory used it, or it was a remnant of a time when the trains stopped more often than they did today. A group of people crowded around several police cars in the parking lot. Louis perked up at the sight.

Brown's hand clamped down even harder on his elbow and he hissed into Louis's ear, "Do not try anything, you understand?" He turned to Emilie. "That goes for you too, Mademoiselle. You try to get into contact with those people in any way and I'll slice open your friend here."

Emilie's voice was even as she spoke in a tone that Louis had never heard from her before. "Message received," she said.

Louis made no move to attract the attention of the people in the parking lot or to move in their direction, but he kept his eyes on the group. Who were they? There were journalists, that was for certain—they stood at the periphery of the group with cameras and microphones. A few police officers were also present, but their eyes were on a figure on the far end of the group, someone Louis couldn't see at the moment. Was it a press conference?

Could it be someone he knew?

Brown released an almost inaudible sigh of relief as they put the group behind them.

Then a voice rose up.

"Hey! Where are you guys going? Do you need any help? Are you wounded?"

"Keep going," Brown said and pushed Louis to increase the pace.

The voice, closer than before, continued, "You sure you don't want any help for your bleeding friend? We have paramedics."

Keeping his face turned away from the man, Blondie replied in a shout, "We're fine. Our car was destroyed, but we don't have much farther to go. Thanks anyway."

A dark-skinned man with a hint of gray in his hair came jogging up beside Louis. "Are you sure?" He wasn't even breathing heavily as he slowed down to walk alongside Louis. "You look like you've been through a lot," he said, taking in the bandage on Louis's forehand and his blood-soaked jeans. "You've got a wound back there, don't you?" He addressed Brown. "Seriously, our paramedics could patch him up in no time."

"I'm sure they have more serious wounds to see to today," Brown said through gritted teeth. "We'll be home in ten minutes."

The man glanced down the tracks and raised an eyebrow. "I'm not sure what state your home is going to be in if it's just ten minutes on foot in that direction." He latched onto Louis again. "Do I know you? You look familiar."

Louis caught sight of Emilie's sundress in his periphery as Blondie drew her along, getting closer to Brown.

"I don't think I know you," Louis said truthfully. He really didn't want to be cut open, so he needed to appear as if he was cooperating. But since Brown was behind Louis, he couldn't see Louis's face. Louis tried his best to convey to the newcomer that he did indeed need help, and that Brown was not a good guy. As they kept walking down the tracks, the black man was soon joined by a blond woman with a camera hanging around her neck.

"What have we got here?" she asked.

The man's eyes never left Louis's face. "Just a bunch of guys walking home, apparently. I thought this guy looked familiar for a moment, but apparently we've never met."

The photographer looked at Louis, looked away, and did a double-take, almost losing her footing on the railway tracks. "You're the mayor's son. What happened to your face?"

The man's eyes widened slightly. He did recognize Louis after all.

The photographer hadn't yet caught on to the general atmosphere of the group, and went on in an excited voice, "Did he come here with his father? He wasn't in the same car. Can I get a picture?" She brought her camera up to her face and aimed it at Louis.

"The mayor's son?" Blondie put a hand on his forehead and slid it down his face.

Keeping his grip on Louis, Brown turned to face the photographer and barked, "Put that thing down. You're not taking any pictures here."

The photographer lowered her camera partway and stared, wide-eyed, at Brown. "Okay…"

The black man, whom Louis surmised was a journalist, seemed to be having a silent conversation with Emilie. The guy had definitely caught on that something was wrong, and must've pegged Emilie as the odd one out. Louis also imagined Gaël was making signals behind Brown's back, because the journalist's eyes darted in that direction several times, a frown forming between his eyebrows.

"Why don't we head back?" the journalist said to his colleague. "I don't think there's a story here. Sure, the guy looks like the mayor's son, but then, so do a lot of people. Dark hair, dark eyes, strong jaw, medium build. It could describe about half the twenty-year-olds in the city."

The camera dangled, forgotten, around the photographer's neck. "But…"

"Come on, let's go." The journalist pulled the photographer to a stop.

Louis's only warning of what happened next was Emilie's disappearance from his line of vision.

Twelve

Blondie flew forward and landed face first between the railroad tracks. This time, Emilie anticipated him not letting go, and went after him, using his own iron grip to bend his arm at a painful angle against his back. With a grunt, he let go of Emilie's wrist, and she jumped back.

At the same time, Louis felt a pull on his elbow as Brown abruptly stopped walking. Louis braced for the inevitable cut, but when it didn't come, he twisted away.

He didn't manage to free himself, but he came face-to-face with Brown, whose neck was trapped by the journalist's arm.

A grunt came from Louis's left—Louis was betting on Emilie attacking Gaël to get him out of the way while Blondie was still down.

"Hey! Over here!" someone yelled. Confusion filled Louis's mind as he realized it was Gaël. "We need help!"

Did he think the police would come to the escaping prisoners' aid? Right now, it looked as though the journalist and Emilie had attacked Brown and Blondie without reason, but the police would see who the actual bad guys were, right?

Still unable to break free from Brown's grasp, Louis decided to push into his captor instead. The unexpected move freed Louis from Brown's grasp, but it also put him in range of the shard of glass. Just as he wondered how he could help out in this fight, the makeshift weapon cut into his thigh.

Gasping in pain, he stumbled back and landed on his ass, straight onto the pointy stones between the railway tracks. It hurt like hell, but not as much as his bleeding thigh.

Emilie had been busy. Gaël lay dazed at the bottom of the far bank of the railway tracks, his chubby face just visible above the grass. Emilie was currently facing off with Blondie, both of them in a fighting stance. Judging by the blooming bruise on his chin and the rip in her dress, they were fairly evenly matched.

Now that Brown no longer had to worry about Louis, he wormed free of the journalist's grasp and downed him with a kick to the knee. The man crumpled with a yell, grabbing onto his leg.

Louis tried to stand up and help the journalist—the fanatic gleam in Brown's eyes, which had been absent during their journey so far, scared him—but he only got to one knee before the pain in his thigh flared again and he dropped back down.

Brown must have decided that he had nothing to gain by attacking a man who was already down, and set off running.

Louis frowned in confusion—Brown was running back in the direction of the city, straight toward the group of people now making its way to where Louis was kneeling.

As Louis recognized the figure at the head of the group, he understood: the mayor of Toulouse had come to inspect the damage from the explosion and show his support. No wonder the photographer had realized so quickly who Louis was; she'd been snapping pictures of his father just a minute before.

Brown must have also recognized the mayor, because he ran straight at him, practically spinning in the air as he grabbed hold of the older man and pulled him a couple of meters away from the rest of the group. He brought the bloodied glass shard out of hiding at last, and up to Louis's father's neck. "Anybody move and I cut his throat."

Everybody froze. A couple of photographers brought their cameras up, probably out of pure reflex, and snapped several pictures.

Now what?

Still on one knee, Louis turned his head at the sound of a grunt right behind him. Emilie and Blondie were still fighting, and Blondie was only a few steps behind Louis. All his attention was on the small girl in front of him. Louis silently cheered Emilie on for giving the large man a run for his money.

With her dress in tatters, she was basically fighting in a sports bra and boxer shorts, but she didn't seem to mind. In fact, as soon as there was a pause in the fight, she ripped the remains of her dress off and threw it to the side, ridding herself of the distraction.

Blondie attacked with a kick to Emilie's legs, but she avoided him with a nimble hop.

Louis figured he ought to help out in the fight closest to him, where he might actually have enough energy to participate, so he fought his way to a standing position, making sure he did so quietly. Though Emilie didn't show it, she must have seen what he was doing—he was standing right behind Blondie, after all.

Emilie launched an offensive, her arms moving so fast Louis didn't even try to follow, and Blondie retreated two steps. Right in front of Louis. Shoving aside his repulsion and figuring this was not the time to try anything fancy, Louis gave the man a good push.

Blondie stumbled forward only one step, but it was all Emilie needed: she threw herself at the big man and landed a sandaled foot square to the side of his head.

Blondie fell to the ground as a low groan escaped him. He curled into a fetal position and stayed there.

Thirteen

"I said, nobody move!"

Brown's scream carried above the sirens blaring in the background—firefighters, ambulances, and police were all swarming the site of the disaster at the chemical factory.

Louis, who remained upright only by sheer force of will, turned in Brown's direction and raised his arms in surrender. He was relieved to see that Brown hadn't cut his father.

"You're all going to stay here," Brown said. "I'm going to take Monsieur le Maire over to the parking lot, and we're going to drive away in one of those pretty police cars. You are not going to call for any reinforcements, or I will shove him out of the car while I'm still driving." He started walking backward, pulling

Louis's father with him. "You let us go and the mayor won't get hurt." He pointed his chin at Louis. "His son can confirm that I do not wish to kill anybody today—unless I absolutely have to."

Everybody turned their gazes on Louis.

He nodded. After all, Brown really hadn't had a use for him today, and had presumably pulled him along only to stop him from contacting the police.

As Brown retreated toward the parking lot with the mayor, Louis looked around without moving his head—right now he didn't even dare that little movement—and spotted Emilie at the back of the group, breathing heavily.

The police officers looked none too happy about the situation, but let Brown and the mayor pass. "Aren't you going to bring your friend?" one of them asked as Brown inched past.

"He'll get a spot in the car if he can walk there himself," Brown replied.

"What about Eric? There were three of you, weren't there?"

So the cop knew about the escaped prisoners from the Saint-Michel Prison.

"You might be able to find him at the Saint-Agne railroad station," Louis said.

The police officer kept her eyes on Brown, but nodded to show Louis that she understood.

As Brown and Louis's father stepped into the parking lot and approached one of the police cars, Louis put down his arms and looked around more thoroughly, searching for anything to help them. Finding nothing, he staggered forward, following Brown and his father.

Brown didn't notice Louis had moved until Louis was a few meters past the group of journalists and police officers.

"What part of 'don't move' didn't you understand?" Brown yelled at him.

Louis didn't register the words. Brown was clearly trying to get Louis's father to open the door of the car, but the old man refused. He must have realized that Brown needed him alive, so he could allow himself a small resistance.

In the end, Brown kept the shard of glass at Louis's father's throat, but let go with his other hand to open the door. At the same moment, a flailing body flew out from behind another one of the police cars. Gaël threw himself onto Brown's back, latching on to the other man for dear life.

Louis ran toward his father. Behind him he heard the pounding feet of what he assumed were the police officers' boots on the asphalt, and the clicks and flashes of the photographers' cameras. Thigh still pounding in pain, Louis ran as fast as he could, shoving the agony to the back of his mind.

By the time he approached the fight, Louis's father was lying on the ground with a widening pool of blood underneath him. Brown had staggered back a few steps, still clutching his shard of glass, and was trying to cut himself loose from Gaël's tight grip.

What was Gaël doing, attacking his idol? Did he think it would convince the police that he was innocent in the events leading up to this moment?

Gaël screamed as Brown sliced his arm, but he didn't let go. "You're not getting away this time, you bastard," Gaël screamed. "You're going to die for what you did to my sister!"

Louis limped his way toward his father's slumped body.

"I don't even know who your sister is," Brown growled as he bit down on Gaël's wrist.

"Sure you do," Gaël countered through gritted teeth. He tried to kick a heel into Brown's groin while straddling his back. "She was the human shield at that jewelry store. If it weren't for you, she would have just gone to prison for a few years. Because of you, she's *dead*. And you didn't even get caught."

"Then why on earth did you help me escape?" Brown sounded genuinely baffled. Louis didn't blame him.

"You have friends waiting for you at the Colomiers train station. It's amazing the number of people you've managed to piss off over the years. They were supposed to make sure you were never seen again."

"You're insane." Brown made another cut to his attacker's arm. His clothes and face were soaked in Gaël's blood, making him look like he'd stepped out of a B-horror movie. Every staggering step brought him closer to the second police car.

Three police officers surrounded the pair, their guns drawn. "You can let go now, *jeune homme*," the female officer said to Gaël. "We've got him."

Gaël's eyes snapped to the woman talking to him, and his mouth fell open at the sight of three guns pointed in his direction. He let go with both arms and legs at once, falling into a heap at Brown's feet.

Brown took off at a run before Gaël had even hit the ground.

A gun fired and Brown pitched forward onto the ground.

Had they killed him? Louis's heart thumped in his chest, and not only from forcing his body to work through the pain.

When Brown rolled over with a groan and clutched his right knee, Louis let out a sigh of relief.

As the three police officers piled on top of Brown, Louis knelt down next to his father. Emilie was already at his side, and was about to turn the mayor over to inspect the damage. The smell of blood was strong, thick, and metallic, and at first Louis was sure his father was dead. He found himself wishing the officer had aimed for Brown's heart instead of his knee.

Louis put two fingers against his father's throat, looking for a pulse. It was there, but Louis didn't have enough medical knowledge to say if it was as it should be. Then he ran his hands across the rest of his father's body—over his face, through his hair, down his arms.

Louis's father opened his eyes, and Louis breathed out a sigh of relief as the familiar eyes, so like his own, stared up at him.

"You're alive." It was a stupid thing to say, but Louis needed to say it. "Where are you hurt?"

"In my leg, I think," his father replied. He closed his eyes and grimaced.

Louis rolled his father onto his back so he could inspect the man's legs, and suddenly a great spurt of blood flew out and hit Louis in the chest. Brown must have cut the main artery.

Louis yelped and clamped a hand over the wound, which was halfway down his father's thigh, and his mind whirled, trying to recall what he'd learned in a first aid class years ago. He needed to make a tourniquet.

"We can use your scarf," Emilie said, and immediately unwound it from around Louis's neck. She brought it down to the wound, and Louis removed his hand for only a second to allow the piece of fabric in. He continued exerting pressure as Emilie wound the scarf around the mayor's leg two times and finished with a tight knot.

The scarf turned red in seconds, but at least he wasn't losing blood in such a spectacular fashion anymore. Just to be sure, Louis kept his hand on the knot and continued to push down on the wound.

"We're going to have matching scars," Louis said to his now unconscious father. He leaned over the old man as his body suddenly remembered how much pain he was in.

When the paramedics took over, Louis used the last of his energy to stagger after them and catch a ride in the ambulance.

Fourteen

Louis shifted carefully on his stool to accommodate his healing wounds. He lifted the bowl of hot chocolate to his lips and savored the smooth feeling of the sweet drink in his mouth. He let out a long, happy sigh.

"Are you sure you're up to going back to class today?" his mother asked from across the table. She wore her usual red-rimmed glasses and colorful clothing—today, a blood-red button-down shirt and a deep purple knee-length skirt. "I don't want you taking any unnecessary risks."

"I'm fine, Maman. So long as I don't do sports, there's no problem. I want to be there for the first class after the school opens up again."

A good part of the city had closed down after the explosion. What Gaël had said turned out to be right; it hadn't been the *poudrerie nationale* that had blown up, but the fertilizer factory right next to it, AZF. Louis shuddered every time he wondered what would have happened if the explosion had caused the *poudrerie* to blow up too. With thirty-one deaths, thousands wounded, and about a third of the city in need of new windows, the disaster was big enough as it was.

Louis's mother studied him over the rim of her coffee cup. "Okay. Good. You've missed enough classes as it is."

Louis's gaze darted to his mother's. "I haven't missed any more classes than the rest of them. The school has been closed."

"So how come you were at Saint-Michel at ten-thirty instead of in class?"

"How did you…?"

His mother opened up a days-old newspaper and slid it across the table to Louis. "The fact that you were not in class was broadcast to the entire city because of this article. I'm sure your teachers have seen it."

Louis sighed. He had skipped *one* class, and everybody knew about it.

"That article is a load of crap anyway," Louis mumbled.

"How so?"

"First of all, they've totally glossed over the fact that one prisoner is still missing." Both Brown and Blondie had been arrested after the fight—along with their chubby helper—but when the police showed up at the Saint-Agne train station, there was no sign of Eric. The man must have rallied after they had left and found a way to get out of the city—or into hiding. Though it wasn't covered in the newspaper, Louis's father had told him that Eric was serving a fifteen-year sentence for robbery with assault. The police were putting a lot of effort into tracking him down, but hoped to keep it out of the public eye.

Louis hadn't been surprised to learn that Blondie's sentence was for armed robbery with attempted sexual assault. Every time he thought of it, he felt the ghost of the man's hand searching his pockets and goosebumps sprang up all over his body.

Brown was in for murder, but had apparently—and luckily for Louis—decided it wouldn't be a good idea to repeat his performance. He'd hoped a peaceful breakout would make the police less eager to chase him down.

"Second," Louis continued, "there's no talk of the link between the breakout and the explosion, though I guess that could be the journalists agreeing to police demands." The *poudrerie nationale* was a high-security location, after all. The fact that someone had made his way in there and caused so much damage apparently hadn't sat well with law enforcement. So, officially, the electrical cabinet that had set everything off was an accident, the result of bad maintenance.

Louis had told the police about Gaël's role in the explosion, but the other man had denied everything. He'd admitted to helping the escaping prisoners once they were out, but claimed he only intended to put them on the right train and then planned to call the police so they could pick them up on the other end. With the confirmation that Gaël's sister had been killed in a robbery years earlier, and his insistence that Brown had been the robber who hadn't been caught, the police hadn't been able to prove that Gaël had anything to do with the explosion. As a result, he faced only a short sentence for aiding the escaping prisoners.

"And finally," Louis said, "they've made it look like I'm the hero." He shoved his finger against the picture at the top of the article. It showed him covered in blood, ready to push Blondie into Emilie's range. The girl was partly visible behind Blondie, but it looked like Louis was the one fighting the man. Even though the journalist had been there, in the middle of the fight, he'd given total credit to Louis. "Emilie and that other guy were the ones who saved the day," Louis told his mother. "I was probably more of a hindrance than a help. I only gave one push."

One corner of her mouth lifting in the beginnings of a smile, Louis's mother glanced at the article. "I guessed as much. You'll have to invite that girl over for dinner soon so I can thank her in person."

"I will." Louis said, both amused and disgruntled that his mother had so little faith in him.

"And saving your father's life is hardly something to be frowned upon."

Louis set down his empty cup and brought a hand up to the black-and-white scarf around his neck. "Thank you for getting it cleaned." By the time the paramedics had removed the scarf from his father's leg, the fabric had been soaked through with blood. His mother must have become as attached to it as Louis, if she preferred to have it cleaned over buying a new one.

"Any time, *chéri*. You take good care of it; you never know when you'll need it again. And you'd better get used to the journalists recognizing you, especially after this. It's a good thing they like you. Better than them searching for something to discredit you at every opportunity, anyway."

"I guess so." Louis drained the last of his hot chocolate and got up—carefully—to set his bowl in the sink.

"You should apologize to your professor for skipping class, Louis."

"Fine, I will," he promised.

He was never skipping class again.

Thank You!

Thank you for reading *The Red Brick Haze*, the prequel to the Tolosa Mystery series. If you liked it, feel free to let other readers know about it.

If you enjoyed spending time with Louis, you should check out *The Red Brick Cellars*, the first book of the series, and look out for *The Red Brick Basilica*, which will be the next one out!

You can find an extract of *The Red Brick Cellars* at the end of this book.

If you want to check out the rest of my stories, drop by my website www.rwwallace.com. I write both long and short fiction, and in most genres.

Also by R.W. Wallace

Mystery

The Tolosa Mystery Series
The Red Brick Haze (free)
The Red Brick Cellars
The Red Brick Basilica

Ghost Detective Shorts (coming soon)
Just Desserts
Lost Friends
Family Bonds
Till Death
Family History
Common Ground
Heritage
Eternal Bond
New Beginnings

Short Stories
Cold Blue Eternity
Hidden Horrors
Critters
Gertrude and the Trojan Horse
First Impressions
Let Them Eat Cake
Out of Sight
Two's Company
Like Mother Like Daughter

Fantasy (short stories)
Unexpected Consequences
Morbier Impossible
A Second Chance

Science Fiction (short stories)
The Vanguard

Lollapalooza Shorts
Quarantine
Common Enemies
Coiled Danger
Mars Meeting

Adventure (short stories)
Size Matters

About The Author

WHEN AZF EXPLODED, R.W. Wallace was taking a nap in her studio on campus. The shaking of the ground woke her up, but after a quick check out the window (the red mushroom-shaped cloud wasn't visible yet), she decided she must have dreamed it and went back to sleep. Her only excitement of the day was managing a call to her parents back in Norway to let them know she was okay before they learned about the explosion on the evening news.

It's not much of a story. So she made up *The Red Brick Haze* instead.

You can find her on rwwallace.com.

Extract of The Red Brick Cellars

THE MOMENT LOUIS set foot in that corridor he would be back in the spotlight. He would be "the mayor's son," expected to mirror his father's opinions and back up whatever policies had recently been passed. He'd no longer be an engineer flitting from one contract and city to the next without a worry in the world; he'd be heir to the Saint-Blancat legacy. He'd be dragged back into politics. Which was why he was standing among tables of food instead of going in to view his father's casket.

The caterers had prepared a feast: everything from shrimp and salmon toasts to sandwiches with duck liver, foie gras, and onion jam. On Louis's right, three tables full of sweets and desserts were refilled by waiters every fifteen minutes. People hadn't come here to eat, but would take a sweet on the way out.

A steady stream of mourners and well-wishers moved up the grand staircase and filed down the hallway to the Salle des Illustres where the casket was displayed.

Louis had been standing there for two hours, working up the courage to go through that procession.

The line of reporters and photographers in the hallway wasn't helping. They weren't allowed inside with the casket, but it was impossible to get in there without passing them. When new mayor Jean-Paul Bousquets arrived half an hour earlier, the cameras had gone off at full speed for a good ten minutes.

How would they treat the deceased mayor's son?

And what would it be like to actually see his father's casket?

Louis still suffered jet-lag from the trip across the Atlantic and felt out of place being back in France after so long in the United States. He hadn't talked much with his mother yet, having arrived late the night before. She had been busy organizing the public wake and the funeral, and was in there right now standing vigil for her husband.

The line of people halted for a moment—someone notable must have stopped to talk to the journalists. A woman stood looking around the room from one step inside the Salle Gervais. Her loose-knit green dress allowed the black t-shirt and leggings underneath to show through. With a wide white belt at the waist, she looked like a cheap synthetic soccer field; an unnaturally bright green with a chalk-white stripe in the middle. Her purple boots were folded down over open laces and long, curly blond hair fell down across a black leather jacket. She must have been melting in that thing; it was supposed to reach 32°C that afternoon.

As the line started moving again, the woman closed her eyes and swayed slightly. When her eyes opened, they turned in Louis's direction. Or rather, in the direction of the food. Taking a deep breath, she eyed the line going into the Salle des Illustres, then her gaze returned to the food.

Once she made her decision, she was systematic and efficient. She made a beeline for the starters and popped three toasts into her mouth while filling a small plate with a variety of delicacies. She grabbed a glass of orange juice and sipped between bites.

Louis smiled. He always enjoyed watching people with a good appetite who took an obvious pleasure in food. Not that this woman looked like she spent all her time eating. She had curves only in the right places.

While she ate what qualified as the main course at this banquet, the strange woman eyed the paintings on the wall behind Louis. Between bites, she found the time to glower at them.

When she passed in front of Louis to attack the desserts, he said, "*Bonjour*, Madame." He brought his hand up to touch his scarf, but of course it wasn't there since he couldn't wear a scarf with a suit.

She frowned at him too—he was apparently no better than Rachou's paintings—but replied, "*Bonjour*." Picking up the last piece from a dessert platter, she mumbled, "Mmm, *pain au chocolat*."

Her English accent was strong, apparent even in those three short words. Come to think of it, her being English would explain the strange clothes. Louis enjoyed the distraction she offered and decided to try making it last a little longer.

"Actually," he said, "since we're in Toulouse, that should be *chocolatines*." The Toulousains had their own word for the classic French treat.

Without turning her head from the food, the woman looked at him out of the corner of her eyes. They were a clear gray-blue and could have been, under other circumstances, very beautiful. But right now, Louis received only ice-cold arrogance. "What's it to you?" they said.

Louis shrugged and suppressed a smile. "You don't approve of the paintings?"

Again, she glanced at him, though continuing to devour pastries from a newly arrived serving tray. After ten years in the States, Louis hadn't lost his accent. It was such an asset for breaking the ice at parties or picking up girls. However, it didn't seem to have much effect on this woman. Of course, if she lived in France, the accent wouldn't be a novelty for her.

The woman wrinkled her nose. "They're a little too… romantic for my tastes."

Louis smiled for the first time in three days. "Well." He bent down as if to tell her a secret. "This is where the weddings used to be performed." He waved a hand toward the three paintings behind him, gloriously illuminated on such a sunny day. "In his paintings, Rachou has depicted love at twenty, forty, and sixty. Eternal love and all that."

The woman finished off her glass of orange juice while she eyed the paintings, then shook her head. "That girl"—she pointed to the *Love at Twenty* painting—"is clinging half-naked to an idiot going off to war. If she loved him, she would let him do what he needs to do and stop whining. If he loved her, he wouldn't be going off in the first place." Those ice-blue eyes darted to meet Louis's gaze, daring him to challenge her assessment. "That woman"—she pointed at the forty-year-old—"is sitting at home doing nothing while I assume her husband is off fighting a war. We're not getting better. And that one—"

How was she going to insult the sixty-year-old?

"—the husband is finally back from war, but this time she's fully dressed and doesn't really look like she cares whether he's there or not. He looks like a statue."

A barrage of flashes going off in the hallway reminded Louis of why he was there, and his smile dropped away. "Well," he said to his English companion, "perhaps we should go into the Salle des Illustres so you can tell me if that is at least more adequate for wedding ceremonies?" And if he could go past the journalists with this strange creature at his side, perhaps she could divert some of their attention.

She eyed the queue inching past and nodded. She set her empty glass on a table and rubbed her hands down each side of her skirt to dry them. "You're allowed to move around?"

"What?" Why should I be restricted to stay here with the food?

She frowned. "You're not security?"

A bark of laughter escaped Louis. A few people in the queue looked their way, but nobody seemed to recognize him. Laughing out loud at his father's wake might not be quite the thing to do. Though his father would most likely have approved. He had requested in his will that they hold a party and dine at his wake.

"You think I look like security?" He smiled at the Englishwoman. "I guess the suit I bought for graduation ten years ago doesn't quite cut it anymore." Louis owned several suits, of course, but they were all in storage back in the States. In his rush to get home, he hadn't spent much time thinking about what type of clothing he'd need.

A blush started high on her round cheeks, but she fought it down quickly as she flipped her mass of blond, curly hair back over her shoulder.

Together they squeezed into the queue in front of an elderly lady leaning on a cane. She didn't seem to mind them cutting into the line. As they started down the hall leading to the Salle des Illustres, Louis offered the Englishwoman his arm and an ironic smile. A sardonic smile of her own graced her full lips and she slipped her hand around his elbow. She emanated a faint scent of lavender, reminding Louis of childhood vacations in Provence.

With only a few meters to go, a journalist recognized Louis. "*Monsieur Saint-Blancat! Quand êtes-vous rentré à Toulouse?*" When did you get back to Toulouse? "What do you know about the mayor's death?" They all turned toward him and flashes went off as though they were the Beckhams at a charity match.

Louis's companion gave him an accusing look, but she kept her head turned away from the photographers, letting her hair cover most of her face. Good, it would give them a mystery woman to look into. Louis curtly shook his head at the journalists, and then they put the paparazzi behind them.

The line of mourners hugged the wall all around the majestic room. The casket stood in the middle, covered in a French flag and the region's Occitan flag. The yellow twelve-pointed cross on red background covered the lower half of his father's casket. A brilliant ray of sunlight slanted in through one of the many tall windows making the cross almost golden.

Before Louis could take in more of the details, a tall police officer blocked his view. Stooping down slightly to look Louis in the eye, he murmured, "*Bonjour*, Monsieur Saint-Blancat. Can I ask you to come with me for a moment? I have some information pertaining to your father's death that I would like to discuss with you."

Find more information about the book on rwwallace.com.

www.ingramcontent.com/pod-product-compliance
Ingram Content Group UK Ltd.
Pitfield, Milton Keynes, MK11 3LW, UK
UKHW022211230426
12048UKWH00016BA/769